GREEN LANTERN

Kilowog's Challenge

adapted by Rob Valois
illustrated by Steven E. Gordon

screenplay by Greg Berlanti & Michael Green &
Marc Guggenheim and Michael Goldenberg, screenstory by
Greg Berlanti & Michael Green & Marc Guggenheim, based upon
characters appearing in comic books published by DC Comics.

PSS!
PRICE STERN SLOAN
An Imprint of Penguin Group (USA) Inc.

PRICE STERN SLOAN
Published by the Penguin Group
Penguin Group (USA) Inc., 375 Hudson Street, New York, New York 10014, USA
Penguin Group (Canada), 90 Eglinton Avenue East, Suite 700, Toronto, Ontario M4P 2Y3, Canada
(a division of Pearson Penguin Canada Inc.)
Penguin Books Ltd., 80 Strand, London WC2R 0RL, England
Penguin Group Ireland, 25 St. Stephen's Green, Dublin 2, Ireland (a division of Penguin Books Ltd.)
Penguin Group (Australia), 250 Camberwell Road, Camberwell, Victoria 3124, Australia
(a division of Pearson Australia Group Pty. Ltd.)
Penguin Books India Pvt. Ltd., 11 Community Centre, Panchsheel Park, New Delhi—110 017, India
Penguin Group (NZ), 67 Apollo Drive, Rosedale, Auckland 0632, New Zealand
(a division of Pearson New Zealand Ltd.)
Penguin Books (South Africa) (Pty.) Ltd., 24 Sturdee Avenue, Rosebank, Johannesburg 2196, South Africa

Penguin Books Ltd., Registered Offices: 80 Strand, London WC2R 0RL, England

ISBN 978-0-8431-9843-0   10 9 8 7 6 5 4 3 2 1

The Green Lantern Corps serves as the keeper of peace, order, and justice throughout the universe. To be chosen to join its ranks is the highest honor and the greatest of responsibilities.

One of the greatest Green Lanterns of all time is named Kilowog. He is an alien from the planet Bolovax Vik.

Every time a new Green Lantern is chosen, it is Kilowog's job to train them and make sure they are ready to perform their duties as Green Lanterns.

One of Kilowog's most difficult challenges came when he was assigned to train Hal Jordan. There had never been a Green Lantern from Earth before.

Hal had been chosen to become a Green Lantern after he saw an alien spaceship crash on Earth.

Its green energy drew Hal to the crash site. Near the spaceship, Hal found a dying alien named Abin Sur. He held out an emerald-colored ring. With his last breath, Abin Sur spoke, "It chose you."

Hal took the ring from Abin Sur and placed it on his finger. A powerful green glow surrounded him, and he suddenly rose into the air.

The ring blasted Hal up into the sky like a rocket and then deep into outer space. Far from Earth, the ring took Hal through a multicolored wormhole. Soon all that surrounded him was the color green.

The next thing Hal knew, he was in a strange-looking alien room. It was like nothing he'd seen before. When he looked down, he saw that his clothes had changed into a green uniform like the one Abin Sur had been wearing.

Someone else was in the room. It was another alien wearing a similar uniform. Hal couldn't believe his eyes. This guy looked a little like a fish!

Tomar-Re led Hal out of the room. Suddenly, they were flying above the strange-looking alien city of Oa. Dozens of Green Lanterns were flying around them. They were each a different alien race.

A new world had opened up in front of Hal's eyes, and it was amazing.

Tomar-Re introduced Hal to the mighty Kilowog. The giant towered over Hal. "Welcome to Ringslingin' 101," he said to the new recruit. "I've never seen a human before. You smell funny."

"I smell funny?" Hal laughed. He couldn't believe that this giant alien thought he smelled bad.

Kilowog began to teach Hal how to use his Green Lantern abilities. "I heard about humans. You think you're the center of the universe," Kilowog said. "If you want to be a Lantern you need to learn fast to look out for the other guy. You need to put the Corps first."

Then, before Hal knew what was happening, Kilowog used his Power Ring to create two giant, glowing fists made out of green energy. "Lesson number one," Kilowog said. "Never let your guard down, poozer."

Kilowog liked to call the new Green Lanterns "poozers"—his word for "rookies." The massive Green Lantern commanded his Power Ring to smack Hal with the glowing fists.

The two giant bursts of energy smashed into Hal and sent him flying.

Hal focused on his own ring, and suddenly a sword and shield appeared in front of him. Without thinking, he charged at Kilowog. But before Hal could get close, the alien used his Power Ring to make a horrifying monster.

"You don't have to be big, but you've got to be smart—and fast," Kilowog grunted.

Hal quickly raised his shield, but the monster easily knocked him to the ground. Kilowog reached out his hand to help Hal up. "Remember, your enemy is not going to play fair," he said.

Hal knew that Kilowog was right. Seizing the moment, he quickly kicked the mighty Kilowog in the chest, sending the giant flying backward. "Me neither," Hal said with a smile. He'd learned his first lesson from his new friend Kilowog.